TASTING FIRE

ESSENTIAL POETS SERIES 92

Guernica Editions Inc. acknowledges
the support of the Canada Council for the Arts.

Canadä

Guernica Editions Inc. acknowledges the financial support of the
Government of Canada through the Book Publishing Industry
Development Program (BPIDP).

ISABELLA COLALILLO-KATZ

TASTING FIRE

GUERNICA
TORONTO·BUFFALO·LANCASTER (U.K.)
1999

Copyright © 1999, Isabella Colalillo-Katz
and Guernica Editions Inc.
All rights reserved. The use of any part of this publication, reproduced,
transmitted in any form or by any means, electronic, mechanical,
photocopying, recording or otherwise stored in a retrieval system,
without the prior consent of the publisher is an infringement of the
copyright law.

Antonio D'Alfonso, editor.
Guernica Editions Inc.
P.O. Box 117, Station P, Toronto (ON), Canada M5S 2S6
2250 Military Road, Tonawanda, N.Y. 14150-6000 U.S.A.
Gazelle, Falcon House, Queen Square, Lancaster LA1 1RN U.K.
Printed in Canada.
Typeset by Selina, Toronto.

Legal Deposit — Fourth Quarter
National Library of Canada
Library of Congress Catalog Card Number: 99-71706

Canadian Cataloguing in Publication Data
Colalillo-Katz, Isabella
Tasting Fire
(Essential poets series ; no. 92)
ISBN 1-55071-090-7
I. Title. II. Series
PS 8555.O425T38 1999 C811'.54 C99-900305-4
PR9199.3.C583T38 1999

Contents

For Concetta, Samantha and Micol
whose passion shapes me

*The rain went sweeping on
in the twilight, spilling moons
on every grass blade.*

Sho-u

Tempus

I

Time catches its breath
between two pillars,
inside, outside:
where chords break
to seek dominion.

In winter moments of sunken hopes.
In summer sparkle of moving waters,

shore to shore,
heart to heart,
too late
as impossible
as too early,
in tenses
perpendicular
to my clarity.

II

We inhabit spaces
at thin angles
distorting shadows
to fit into time warps,
systems we conjure up
for our own amusement
in sleepdream days and nights:

kisses that say I love you,
letters that say I love you almost,

hands weave the face of time
ascribing to the day
its tattered reflection.

Kisses

For Giuliana

I
White Kisses

The first kisses were a diaphanous light drawing down my spirit.

Only after she took off her white wedding dress, did she allow him his first passionate kiss.

He, who had dared to steal a kiss after their first walk alone so many months before, waited by the bed. His eyes full of yearning. He began to kiss her hands, remembering the night when she had rejected his stolen kiss.

It was a moonlit December night. A brooding darkness surrounded their footsteps, softened by the hazy light of a waxing moon. They were hurrying to get inside the gates of her courtyard before her father locked them out.

Laughingly she warned him to watch his step, "There are potholes!"

Then she mistepped and fell clumsily into his arms.

He laughed and stayed her fall.

Her face turned away from the moon, softly cursing the tricks of darkness.

Holding her steady, he tried to plant a seedling kiss on her flushed cheek.

She slapped him hard, with a twinkling ready hand. "Don't do that again!"she said in her mother's stern voice. Her clear eyes full of dismay, her sculptured lips, unsmiling.

The sound, like a knife slicing the quiet night, stopped him cold. He never tried to kiss her again. Until tonight.

This was their wedding night. As his kisses rained on her hands and cheeks, he banished forever, her long ago rebuke from his heart.

Their kisses began like raindrops, moving into stormy explorations of breath, body and mind. They called to me in blue magnetic longing.

My spirit began to spin, in a humming, circular motion towards the cyclone eye of their passion, into a core of razor blue light. Their kisses grew beyond their skin, spinning parabolas of white atoms, snakeround, drawing sibilant currents of cosmic vectors into their merging forms.

The light sang to me, reaching for me as their kisses grew more passionate. From the skin of desire to the act of penetration and union, parabolas of cosmic geometries, scintillating atoms, merged into the twining forms of man and woman. A pyre of magenta flames enveloped their bodies, illuminating the dark stone room at the foot of snow-capped mountains.

I became aware of gentle voices whispering to me along corridors of roseblue light. Then, a milk light tunnel opened, forged by kisses becoming sweat, fluids and energy. My waiting spirit began its descent, like a kite drawn to the flow of scurrying winds, inexorably pulled into earth's weighty gravity, into the heart of a long blue cone.

Time waves moved in a vertigo of delight. The crescendo of kisses called to me. My spirit moved towards the churning tunnel, seduced by the white cone of light spinning out from their lovemaking bodies. Closer to their passion, as soundless as falling snowflakes, I fell into the earth's trance, into the secret spiral of time and space, my descent as conscious as the sound of winds moving through forests.

Excitement aroused my spirit, growing into a forceful knowing, a solid destiny. Carefully conscious, my soul took care to notice each moment of passage as my human spirit moved steadily into their circle of light, their sweet kisses a beacon of hope.

Soon, I would have a new body.

II

Dark Kisses

I am tiny. I am kissing my skin. It feels salty. Smells of earth and dry summer sun. I smell and suck and kiss my arms. When I finish loving my skin I walk from the sunny balcony into the shaded kitchen where my mother is making dinner. I creep up behind her, like a cat stalking a bluebird.

She does not notice me.

I want to touch the back of her long summer skirt. I long to touch and kiss her summer brown skin, bury my head against the salty skin of her legs.

She moves slowly around the stove. Has not yet seen me. Lately she has gotten fatter, rounder, slower; I no longer fit into her lap. She rarely holds me now and I miss the cradling that makes my body shiver with joy.

I am starved for the smell and touch of her skin, for the touch of her warm arms and lips.

When she finally notices me she asks if I have come to help her. I want to help. She asks me to bring bread from the side board to the dinner table. I pile long slices of thick, brown bread into a flat plate and walk towards her, tottering slightly.

She comes towards me smiling,"It's too heavy for you," she says taking the plate from my hands. She notices the bright red marks dotting my arms like angry snake bites. Grabbing my arms she begins to scream.

11

I try to bolt. Screech at her.

In the struggle of tangled shouting she drops the plate of bread. In slow motion, bread and earthenware scatter over the green marble floor. Roughly, she pulls me close to her watermelon belly. Her face has changed from smiles to fear. Concern, sorrow, pain cross her face like storm warnings.

My shoulders shake under the weight of her hardening voice.

I begin to cry. Hot tears fall in a flood of angry pain. I can no longer make sense of what she's saying. The menacing scent of fear penetrates my heart, soaking my mind with scalding anger. Furious and helpless, I begin to screech again. This time, louder.

She squeezes my arms like stubborn pomegranates as I struggle to get free.

"Why do you suck your skin like that?" The violence of her question stirs more terror and confusion.

I break free, howling with rage, stumbling over the broken plate of bread. Bits of bread and tears fly around the gleaming floor. My legs kick at the mess as I run from her elemental anger.

A sliver of sharp crockery flies up to cut her leg. She gasps. Breaks into wild, thundering sobs. Runs towards her bedroom leaving a thin trail of blood on the shiny floor.

Wild with pain I continue to whimper, licking at the tears falling on my burning arms. My tears seem to soothe me a little, calm my confusion.

I notice an angry red halo around my own tiny suck marks. My mother's venom on my naked skin. My tears fall heavily now, cooling my wounded skin with the deliberate cadence of rain bathing my mother's red carnations growing on the balcony. Fat tears pool around the red marks of her anger, around the red marks of my love. For a long time, I stand in the empty kitchen waiting for her fingermarks to disappear from my arm, moaning like a wounded animal, waiting for my tears to glide under my skin, for their watery balm to quench the flames of rage, listening to her angry sobs swelling in the sunlit air.

Fig Tree

For Diodato

See how the fig tree
reaches to sunbreath,
birdwing of sky,

city fig tree
imported
through threads of time.

Immigrant timewarp
in exiled land,
binding
the sacrificial
themes of his life:
the garden
the house,
the family womb,
where all dreams are possible,
if you close your eyes
to the pine tree faces.

Heartspace

For Adriana

today
my father's heart
beats a fine
steady heartbeat
gone is the fear
that brought his racing heart
to the dim corridors of death

he's won the race
for a while
his clear eyes
and steady will
carry on

resting in a foreign bed
waiting for the evening news
for a grandchild's soft caress

his heartbeats remember
the golden wheatfields
he harvested at twenty
before the war made him
angry and homeless
the songs of mountain birds
and whispering serpents
his tired eyes lifting
from the plough
to catch the long trainwhistle

filling the pilgrim air
and as he falls asleep
his heart remembers
a slow wagon headed homeward
and the scent of fragrant bread
waiting by a steaming bowl
of summer vegetables

My Mother's Poem

For Concetta Sinibaldi

She leans into her pain
closer and closer to its
clawing blindness —
a growing darkness
on a wide starry plain.
She picks up her pen
and stabs at the face of pain
grown long horned
and hungry over
long years.

Among waves of thoughts
washing up
on the shores of her life
wounding images,
glinting swords
pierce her days and nights

She writes
in the old dialect,
stringing words together,
rare jade
on a strong white thread.

Her memories a relief,
a fresh breath
shaping the theme of her poem:
her lost youth

and the violent removal
from the womb of her mountains
after the war,
the loss of her people,
their shared language
and lost dreams.

I can barely make out
her writing — she has written
in some kind of shorthand.
I ask her to read it out loud,
the pasta bubbling
in the Sunday pot
is boiling
over.

As she reads the words,
images form in the ears
of my first language,
village smells rise
through forgotten sounds:
vespers chiming at sunset
the trill of croaking frogs
old kitchen voices
crackling stories
around winter fires
the dusty roads
we walked together
me holding her hand
so long ago.

Her heart becomes a lava
pouring out quiet words

against the sobbing
October rain.
The old dialect
bubbles in my soul
like an untasted
vegetable,
aching
against my heart,
opening up
channels of words.
I want to say,
"I like it.
You are a fine poet,"
but the praise won't come.

She closes her notebook
and returns
to the Sunday cooking
stirring silence
into food.

Suspended
in the spell of haunting
images, clutching
her green notebook,
my mother's poem churns
through my fingers
like an ancient rain.

The Sound of a Distant Wailing

For A.C.

I

Parts of my childhood
fall away
in a slow reel
of backwards
images
unwinding
to a final scene
as each old relative
moves reluctantly
into death's watchful shadow
disappearing
from the very photographs
we keep in dusty closets
taking them out
from time to time
to remember the way we were
and looked, and laughed
in other times and places.

The faces of the dead ones dim
in the photograph album
surrounded by old documents,
faded papers attesting
to our acts of transition
from there
to here
to now

where we find ourselves
once again
burying our dead.

II

To her I give back
these memories:
to this stubborn aunt
who moved undaunted
through three continents,
always courageous
always smiling.
Her small, stout body
fine cropped hair
and deep, grey eyes,
trailing a wistful smile
in a mix of Italian dialect
and the Buenos Aires Castellan
from her years
in Argentina
where, alone,
she raised two children
after her husband's
slow death,
polluted lungs
bringing his final silence.

For years
she sat lonely
on a small, rough bench
in a suburban Toronto garden,
fragrant with flowering pear trees,
watching for early roses

as she rested from her work.

She raised three
Canadian grandchildren
with no English.
With easy love she taught
them hybrid latinate sounds,
tollerating their harsh shaped
Saxon words at the dinner hour,
understanding little of their chatter.
In our scattered family
she was an elder,
one of the few remaining.
In her last years
as fragile as a lonely
twig, whose stubborn leaves
are wooed away
by the whispering
promise of hurrying winds.

And one day,
like a withered leaf,
she fell on the stonehard
April ground ,
never again to return
to the warm spring garden.

III

The graves at Holy Cross
are filling up. Rows
and rows of resting places
mark immigrant names
at the edge of a foreign city.

From here the hapless dead
look down on the merciless city
that took their dreams,
used up their memories
ate up their lives like bitter bread
to the moment of final breath.
This is the last port holding
a thousand immigrant bones;
yet no sign remains
of their tired days
and struggles.
In neat rows and depths,
in solitary arrangements:
friends, family, neighbours
lie in permanent sleep.
It's hard to find
an uncle, friend or cousin
whose bones lie weary,
unless someone
more familiar
points to the spot.

IV

April again.
The sky fills up with lark songs.
The day is cloudless and dry
as we follow the coffin.
Zia is finally buried,
in a grand mausoleum
(a gift from her grieving children),
never again to return,
to the dulling sounds
of the garish city,

where our brief lives survive
like short spring blooms.

Another funeral is done.
There have been three or four
this year, all members of our
family, and not all old —
just weary and empty of light.

V

Today,
another funeral
moves among the graves
in a quiet shuffling of tears.
Muffled wails rise from
knots of black bandannas
hiding the sallow, solemn faces
of dark eyed, weeping women
prayer beads move
through work worn fingers
Sunday shoes,
worn like slippers, shuffle
past the slippery grass.

The men, walking in sober pairs,
carry the burden of pain
in a shield of silence
against secret tears.

The dead do not awaken
to the soft crying
to the murmur of ancient prayers.
Even when the living

mumble their names,
in old dialects,
the dead say nothing.

The dead no longer hear
the slow, slender syllables
bounded by sorrow and pain.
It is the living who remember
the countless voyages
the constant partings
the endless journeys
from homeland
to foreign port
to now.

VI

Larks circle overhead.
Soundless wingbeats stir
the trundled air;
worms burrow inward
tearing the earth's deep flesh.

In this place of frozen dreams,
far from their village homes,
the mourning, doleful songs
of wailing, black robed women
chanting death's unwelcome
coming, is quietly remembered.

The silence is remarkable.
It reminds me of the crucifixion
scene in Pasolini's *Gospel
According to St. Matthew*

where the absence of sound
amplifies the black and white
imagery, making death's lament
more poignant, in the gaping
throats of the living.

Here, in this place —
in this flat Canadian meadow —
the wailing sound
of rural, southern towns
seems absent;
lying inside
the living
and the dead
like a lost dream.

VII

On an ordinary Saturday in April
the hushed Canadian ritual
is played out,
new and unformed,
the unborn rite
of a lost tribe.

The quiet shuffle
of bedroom slippers
trembles against
the crackling sound
of a rogue wind,
fingering stiff
black clothes.

The image unfolds in a filmy
glaze over the soundless landscape.

Two crows watch
as the one legged woman
who was our aunt, mother,
grandmother,
sister and friend,
is laid to rest
in the curve of this wild,
green land, she never really knew;
alive only in our memories
and fading photographs.

The image freezes
in the crow's curious eye
hovering in the vast, blue sky.

And in the depth of this photograph,
in this moment of utter stillness,
stirring in the soundless,
eyeless years,
I hear
the faraway sound,
the persistent,
echoing cry,
swelling
and immutable:
the sound
of a distant
wailing.

Pain and Possibility

For Janice Doherty

I

So this is stagefright,

while the moon ripens
to harvest yellow
and the wandering wind returns
to wash away the strength of sunshine,
like a house reflecting
the quality of life lived inside me,
I feel the noisy or quiet days
the patterns of sun and rain
moving through dusty rooms.

Thoughts leap at me
conjuring up old voices,
reminding me of moments
when hands touch
in parting,
the sorrow of beginnings
posing as joy.

II

Waiting for the new circle
to take me in,
for a winter to embrace me,
for its tenderness to hold my silences,
I long for a new fire,
a bursting sun,

a brilliant, starry sky,
invisible to mortal eyes
but deeply felt by those
who sense the call.

III

I feel my new life,
a simmering
wavelength,
a tempered prayer
sipped from a silver goblet,
refreshing the self.

IV

Behind me,
the road fills up
with misted mornings,
offering me
the loneliness of courage,
the trust of busy hands.

Before me,
another morning opens,
whispering new secrets.

Why do I fear
to walk into its warm embrace?
Does it not hold the same dreams
that have guided me
on the long road back?

I know the path to freedom
is never the same

no matter what the masks.

Today,
my heart feels
strong and wise,
changing days
open before me,
an unexpected gift
already given.

Herald of the Coming Good

For Giovanni Colalillo

It is the sound of your space. Eveningtime. Perfumed
 honeysuckle
and wild orange. Aztec rug, silent as buddhic planes.
 Rock music
stirring the sentimentality of sex centres. From an
 open window,
a furry cat intimates cosmic pleasures — white moon
 mice in butterfly
formations. Drifting piano notes parade the sadness.
The eighteenth soul lulls itself to heaven. A long day
 of neurotic metaspaces.
Swishing nightsounds caress my body. Invisible
 moonbeams weave bony poems.
Tired hands wither. Gurdieff smiles at my smile. I
 align myself to modern voices
— Fourché, Di Cicco, Ginsburg. Gurdieff's
 moustache tugs wildly at my soul:
handlebars of the fourth way soaring in metaspheres.
My grandfather looked like him, though its hard to
 divide the masks.
Telling old tales, he wandered through timewarps
 clothed in roaring fireplaces.
We played games only white holes remember:
children inventing the Game of Thought, inspiring
 The Tirade of Poetry.
His weaver's hands holding inviolate symbols.
Colours shaping the tone of his cosmic words.

He who, one afternoon, placed a book by my seven
      stones and taught me
the art of being windborne, of listening to white
      witches in village wells.
He invented all the symbols, fashioned my beads of
      knowledge, carved journeys into my skin.
These are secret spaces inside me.
I know them through webs of stardust where angels
      weave the silver thread of Self,
the bluegreen fire of oceans. I know the secret words.
I drink dark liquors. Talespinning is the ancient,
      witching craft of my spirit.
To those who see, I reveal my tapestry of lies, the
      spin of Light, the pendulum of Thoughts.
I invoke magic cocoons of lifeblood: Whitman,
Rimbaud, Hesse, Christ, Harpies of Orpheus,
Shiva and Kali, water and fire, Tarot, Yod, Vau, Heh,
Sephiroth, tree, South African violence,
coffeecups of dead Salvadorian babies.
We are caught in starships of venom and desire.
Our duty as scribes the improbable dilemma.
Wanting to know, to do, to act, to make true.
How deeply do we care for matter? Eyes see.
A hurrying pen holds fast the world.
Frantic hands glide through webs of stars: a chrysalis
      in orbit.
Causation as effort of expression.
Transition. Chaos. Nowness.

November 1956

For Emily P.

I have never felt
so close to my childhood
never seen myself
so compressed in time
never so clearly glimpsed
in my mind's dark corridor
the image of a dull grey street
in late November

small feet walking
through cold toes
eight-year-old eyes
tasting the wonder
between wide
winking snowflakes
floating in the chill
blue air
of a new country.

Samantha on a Winter's Night

you run into the room

it is nearly midnight

I have watched your body
change from child to woman
in the space of a few hard years

bouncing your youth
into this winter's evening
you are moonlike

a shy smile betrays
your coming womanhood

only my pen
weaves the moment
into this poem
your budding soul
sounding
your sacred
loveliness

Birthing

For Mariella

I

today
my sister
alone
you
gave birth
a corner of the night
hid your cries

II

sipping jasmine tea
in a downtown cafe
I taste the pain
of your labour
feel the river of
your joy

III

today
another sister
has blown
the universe
through the thighs'
thin crack
heaving
the crying breath

of a new child
harvesting
mouthsful of air
in a new sowing

IV

a sonseed
suckles
her breast
fondling her soulparts

she thinks his name
and marks his space

V

when a man is born
the silence is unprepared
for what follows
hands welcome
the child to stay
echoing warmth
and softness

VI

a mother's hands
string him
like a bead
time traps his wings
he is earthbound
earthfired

VI

though he may never
know
how her passion invoked
his hunger
tonight
his mouth
hungers for his mother
for the taste of life
is strong
the taste of love
is wild

Faith

For Micol

For that which unites all life is passion.
Kierkegaard

On the tenth day of September
in the year 1797
a woman
aged thirty-six years
to her compatriots known
as Mary Wollstencraft
died in childbirth.

Midwives warmed the child's blue body.

Keening sisters
in midnight hours
looked on
eyes clear with understanding.

In her youth
she had shown great promise
expressed wild opinions
in *The Vindication of the Rights of Women,*

and though few could read her words
or express strong disapproval
in high places
her words and courage
were dismissed,

Her message
re-absorbed in time's eternal veil
to re-awaken with new women
in other time experiments.

It was morning when they closed her eyes
swallows soared above grey clouds.
Out of the pollution of the ages
her soul went back
to where dreams are
attended by a million
singing angels
bearing white camellias
where she waits in hope
smiling at the passionate
dreams of her sisters.

Feminist Frame

For Samantha

I have no time for women
who stay thin for their men
for the approval of shop clerks
for the images offered by *Vogue*
for the dark envy of their friends
for the torturing maintenance of a body
they might have had at fifteen
for the stifling despair of growing larger
and wondering if they'll be despised.

I have no time for women
who spend their lives counting calories
munching greens like dull spring cows
women who waste away their lives
thin sticks of despair
quietly haunted
unripened
afraid to become something
beyond a thin body frame.

Thin women
turning into whispers
lingering
between grim lives
serving themselves up as images
for the greedy eyes of others.

Shadow women
who repress their sublimity
deny their codes of power
become martyrs to the cause of slavery.

Quiet termites
hidden from daylight
inventing the architecture of destruction.

The women I have time for
are clear and unbounded
centred in their struggle of becoming
embracing the nourishment of days.
Whether fat or thin
their aim is to occupy space
serving up their passion
to be themselves
their ultimate appetite
their great hunger
is to be more
more always
themselves.

Grandmother's Photograph

For Vincenzo Pietropaolo

I know her only from her black and white photograph. Grandmother is a tall woman surrounded by three of her seven children. One died as a baby, before the time of the photograph. The three who are missing are not yet born. Her husband is in the photograph too, along with her eldest son, middle daughter and youngest daughter who is about two. This child is cherubic, with the ancient face of a baby in a Mediaeval painting. She is beautifully dressed, in a light chiffon dress of unknown colour. She is grandmother's spitting image.

In grandmother's short life — she died at fifty three of ovarian cancer — oppression, poverty and loneliness were her constant companions. If she tasted joy and ease, no one will ever know. If she shared her sorrow with friends, who will tell? No one who knew her has ever said much about her inner life, least of all her two surviving sons, both born after the photograph was taken. My father was her last child, and because he was twelve when she died, too young to be aware of sorrows that go beyond the self, he seems to have no intimate knowledge of his mother's inner world. He remembers only the pain of her abandonment, the anguish of his orphanhood. He remembers well that her life was hard. But I know this only in a generic way, can only interpret her suffering from the painful tone in his voice, the resigned look on his patient face. But even here there is a space I cannot touch or explore to my satisfaction. I long to know how hard it really was for her; how she felt and thought and dreamt as a woman raising six children on her own through those long years, never knowing when her husband might appear or disappear from their life. Her husband, the itinerant storyteller, sometime carpenter, and world traveller was hardly ever at home.

Family history tell us that, in fact, grandfather was not with her when the photograph was taken. They say that she had the photograph taken with money he sent from America, that she sent it to Boston where he went after serving in the First War. In Boston, he paid someone to paint his own photograph into the portrait, so he could stand with his wife and children. When he returned home, a few years later he brought her a large photograph showing a full family portrait. It is this doctored photograph, grandfather is standing to the right of grandmother looking like the sort of husband and father who was always around. They are standing well apart, shoulders never touching. Grandmother's lonely life is as transparent as his own.

Her years of married life were hard. Each day started early, often before sunrise, stirred by the sounds of crying children. When you have children you don't sleep in. Most days, the cock crowed after she was already up. She could hear the muffled voices of dark men shuffling under her balcony like morning shadows, moving towards faraway fields or mountain sheepfolds.

Her dark hair, always dishevelled in the early morning, is combed high on her head in the photograph, two long curls frame her oval face, short, wispy bangs cover her forehead. She is wearing her best clothes, not exactly smiling, looking neither happy nor sad. A neutral look of endurance dances in her eyes. She seems to be looking past the photographer, far away, beyond her life of young children and absent husband. She may be daydreaming, imagining another life for herself.

In the 1920s, in the peasant villages of southern Italy, family photographs were rarely taken, so this must have been a special occasion for her, an opportunity to relax from her gruelling life, a chance to briefly claim her identity. To reflect and shine.

To dress up, comb your hair high and look away into the distance must have been a great holiday for you, grandmother.

How I wish I knew more about you. Though I try, I can't really imagine how hard and lonely your life must have been. It's no wonder you died young and alone, without any support from your husband, who was far away in Australia when you died on a warm June day in 1934. They say he did not find out about your death until months later. I wonder who was with you when you died.

In the only photograph we have of you, you look young and strong, a woman of great pride and courage. We can't see the cancer growing in your ovaries that took your life. A tragedy, they said, just like your husband's mother who died of "women's troubles" when her son, your husband, was only five. In choosing you as his bride, did grandfather ever dream you would die so young? Did he ever once think you would forever abandon your five children into each other's care, under the watchful eyes of relatives, until he returned from Australia that Christmas? Probably not. Though life histories are circular, no-one expects to suffer twice what they have endured once. Certainly grandfather had no notion of your cancer when he left three years earlier.

In the photograph you were in full bloom. They say there was no hint of the dark cancer growing in your blood until the day you died. Father says you did not know how sick you were. He says that the doctors did not diagnose you properly and there was no cure for you when they began to suspect your problem. Besides you felt fine most of the time. Only a bit more tired than usual, a little more pale.

Grandmother is in her thirties when this photograph was taken just after the First Great War. The two older children, who are about seven and five, look distant, unconcerned, as if waiting for the photographer to be finished. Her husband looks guarded. Her youngest daughter looking older than her few years, stands resolutely in front of her mother, a faint smile on her round, pale face. This angelic daughter died at twenty five, a year after her mother. An infection, born of a miscarriage, took her young life, leaving her only daughter motherless. In the photograph, she is standing on a chair, slightly to the left of her mother, looking bright and innocent, her sweet face as beautiful as grandmother's. Like a sturdy shield, she stands before her mother's tall frame as if to protect her — Maria Malatesta, our fallen warrior.

Song for the Beloved

her eyes, her eyes
luminous stars
rustling
evening breezes
brown slices
of light awakening
the voice of distant stars

her eyes, her eyes
mountain lichen
holding
the scrolls of the universe
DNA of watery skins
she picks up a single stone
and touches it to her tongue

morning disrobes
under snowy stars
a wild song hides
in a sparrow's open wing
stirring the dreaming rain

she brings wildroses
to our breakfast
her skin fragrant
with gardens

my hands sprout
new courage

words ripen between us
and in her eyes
a shadow whispers
when was I more than now,
when was I less by dying?

Lorca Writing

For Stratis

"Careful," says Lorca,
white beard brushing
the tip of his scratching pen.
Words spill on a scrap of paper
he's saved just for this day.

"Careful, careful," he mumbles,
waving his pen like a bloody sword,
at the boyish wind ruffling his hair,
"Life is not a dream."

His heart bent to the task of writing,
he pushes through cloven words
wordspirits cluster around him
like a thousand flying fish.

"What am I writing?" he wonders
scratching his craggy chin,
"Careful, Lorca, careful," warn the words,
"Writing can end your life."

The Old Man

For Cristina

His old, wizened face turned towards the hills. Beyond the wide river, the sun, barely round, peeked through the morning mist, a yellow gourd brightening the morning dew. The old man's jaws tightened against his pounding heart, against thoughts and words that whispered to him like midnight ghosts. Too much pain, too much fear. He turned to the sunlight hoping it would melt away the icy coldness coursing through his body.

From his train seat he saw peasants curved over interminable rice paddies, their slim bodies bending away from sunlight. He felt their pain, felt the hands of pain clawing at his back. Was his own life not like theirs, working from dawn to dusk, often later, bent over his tiny rice field like an old willow twisting its face to the river? He knew the way of pain: how pain sought out more and more places in the body, pulling, pushing, tearing through muscles and nerves, curving the back until he forgot what it was like to be young and lithe and upright. Pain, poverty and hard work were the constant companions of his days

His old, blinking eyes brimmed with sorrow as the train crossed the wide plain with the speed of a hurrying dragon.

Spring again. The land awakens. New life burns in luminous greens. Hope.

The old man, feeling raw and shrunken, lifts his gnarled hand across his face to relieve an itch. His wrinkled hands are the hands of someone whose body has long worked with a rhythm that swallows up the soul.

As the morning train speeds past the rice paddies, the old man struggles to push away a clutch of feelings that threaten to explode in the very centre of his memory. Outwardly he maintains a strong, impermeable presence. Someone passing by his seat might notice a resolute man, old and proud with some sort of important business in town.

He struggles against clawing feelings that threaten to overwhelm him. He gazes at the sun's face, grazing the edges of the misty horizon.

His spirits lift somewhat as he watches the sunrise. His churning feelings project his daughter's face in his mind's fitful eye. He sees her dancing, young and carefree, a bright fairy against the sun's ascending roundness. Her long black hair gleams like a comet's tail in the wind, her dainty feet move in a graceful, morning dance.

"No," he thinks, raising an old hand to shield his eyes from the vision. "I have no daughter. And if I once did, she is no longer mine. She who was my daughter now belongs to another." Wracked by pain, he can't bear the weight of tears falling on his burning cheeks. He hides his face from the probing sun eye. The train whistles across the valley.

"I don't remember a daughter," he mutters between sobs. "I am dreaming that I had a daughter and in this dream I imagine I'm a man with a daughter." His mind forages for new images in the aching archives of memory. His wise heart tells him not to, warning him against these dangerous memories, warning him not to remember where he has been and what he has done. His heart tells him to imagine another man someone other than who he has become, suggests he abandon the tide of memories that can only bring him pain. Aware of his heart's bidding, he pushes forward into the valley of his fertile imagination. Ah, yes, now he remembers . . . he once knew an old man, knotted and gnarled like him-

50

self, who had a beautiful young daughter. She was the moon and sun of his life. This man had been able to keep his daughter. Yes, this man had worked from sun-up to sun-down, breaking his back to support his child, to keep her from being sold into the kind of slavery faced by young women whose parents were too poor to keep them.

That other man, who reminded him of himself, had never taken his daughter to town, never sold her for the price of a young calf.

That man delighted in his daughter's beauty, which grew with each passing day. That man had never faced the kind of drought and starvation that, eventually, deprived him of his meagre living so he could no longer feed himself and his child. That man had not gone hungry, never begged for help. That old man had never been shamed and humiliated by his more prosperous neighbours. His neighbours had never turned away from his need.

That other man had never gone to market and sold his daughter to a man who had chained her to his cart like an animal. He had never walked away with enough gold for two spring calves if he wanted them, gold enough to buy a fresh supply of seed for his tiny rice field, to buy food in the event of another drought, to get new tools to repair the hut's leaky roof. No, that man, had not done any of these things. Offering his last bowl of rice to his child, he had gone hungry, sucking in air and chewing his tongue when hunger grated at his body. That man had even risked his life, going out under cover of darkness to steal a few grains of rice for his daughter or begged in the street for some grains of rice.

But he had never sold his dignity. Had never bartered his flesh and blood in order to survive.

His pain and sacrifice during the long, unwavering drought rewarded him with the gift of his daughter's beauty and youth. Barely thirteen, as lovely as a sun maiden, she danced for him at the end of each hungry day, sharing her encouraging smile with her dying father as if he were still young, still strong and lithe and carefree.

An Ancient Way of Dancing

For Sandra and Sherri

come
let us dance
let us put on
the music
and dance in ancient ways

let us climb
the air with spiral stepping

let wide skirted
women become naked
put on masks and shed
the guise of slavery
with music and colours
let us face dark mirrors
warm the lips
move the hips
unfold our shrunken hearts
through morning sunrays
and moontime rhythms
dance for a new awakening

sing for the drumbeat
that won't let go

dance through me
says the sorrow
dance past me

say the memories
reclaim me
whispers the body
move that still point
cry the voices

dance between the shadows
see us from a new point of view

women uniting in circles
sisters dancing together
dancing in ancient ways
in the wise
new ways of spirit

*The title of the poem is the title of a painting by Inuit artist, Ikseetarkyuk.

Dzikir

There is no reality outside the reality of God.
Sufi Chant

Consider. Spice coriander. Evening moon.
Glass reflecting sweet music.
Bach interludes at dawn
Arpeggio notes. Piano escaping moonless bends.
Setaceous memories.
Fireplaces. Stories the mind to itself repeats.
Wordblooms clinging to wine.

Flagwaving crowds in 1940 swastikas.
Reversed mythologies in thimble drops of evening
nectar.

Window frost seeping from fingers to waiting
mouths.
Melting glaciers.
A trek to a nordic river.
The I am presence in each.
Superconscious mountains, templed and graced.

Windplaces loosening.
Clamouring, eyeroving images balancing the world.
Translucent cemeteries in rows of skull grins.
Gunfire at dusk.

Breathing mindfulness
Spaced-in-visionaries
Spiced fingers turning old pages

Pages that appear to be gold rimmed
Glorious days of time past,
time future and time possible.

The denial of time.
Womb-whore phrases we swallow.
Past perfect exits.

Symbols in ice,
Lingering wholeness, of when, where, then.
Wholism impact. Rememberings.
Here and now suchness.
Shaped wilfulness.
Corruptible passions.

The bluishness of flames crackling a sadness.
The strength of sadness. The strength of sadness
rippling.

A sparkling, artful room in German
occupied France.
A wrinkling face.
A faded turquoise gown retreating in
old slippers.

Lapsed elegance.
Sadness roving crevasses of faces.
The smile forgetting the joy.
The erasing of patterns.
The Being-in-Death.
The slaps of life on bony canvases.
Laced poses of reconstructed soul images.

Dreamfulness.

Damnation.
Materialism in a back pocket.
Irate December quarrels with shadows.

Morning.
Again the light captures fraying notes. Lingering
  music.
Orange symphony under raving paintbrushes.
Devotion.
The almost found wild roses.
Blue petals dancing in a crystal vase.

Bleak curtains longing for the caress of leaves.
Leaves longing for sunshine.

Lovers. Mouth to mouth love
Wild incantations billowing in blades of grasses.
A tabernacle of wildflowers filling the hands.
The still pale moon moving through fire.

Cries.
A gemmifereous desert.

Gehenna.
Word mute a litany. Remote.
Mouthless.

Invented, succulent fields gasping late
      spring light.
Inward sensing. Speculative embers.
Magic felling falsity.

The truthing of gender.

City rooves, imploring nightsounds (BLEEP! Shriek!!!
BEEP. Screeching, horny moths. Hey You!).

The white madness of fraying moonbeams,
and the dogeared distraction of paradigms.
The simulated telepathy of computers.
The nuclear articulation of pogroms.
Polish-American parables clothed in popevison
      mentality;

The continuity of verbs crouched in a paraphernalia
      of charms.
Everywhere the civilised

Omar Mukhtar eating desert sands in weary chains,
betrayed by Fascist uniforms in glittering palaces
Libyan conspiracies in color commercials.

Men/women/wooing causative images, lying in
      subjunctive dreams of
damnful dress designers. Clothed
      men/women/copulating d i s t a n c e s
Post modern terrorists.
Heresies of statehood.
Searing embers of Nothings
in dry clever smiles.

To Dante from 1981

We are oft
without centre
computerized
in the medulla oblongata
of living.

Suffering poets of life . . .

What are stars but light?
Oeneric waves of eternal flow,
to our eyes
a great Becoming
among Beings of wisdom

the universe
unfolding
in rose petals
of Light.

Gnostica

Had we known then how magic
engages bluebells in flights of light,
how seas murmur in the spine of seashells
and beaches run to pine trees
in Tuscan landscapes. How love
flew out of your coffee pot and dared me
to dream of kisses.

Had we known then how passion
folds up like a penknife and hands
sprout love anew. How clocks stop timing
lifewaves, and south sea wars bring
death and pain and wise unknowing.

And shall I take it back all that I said to you?
How you doubted Spring perverting my questions,
squaring answers to the run of circles,
concluding poems without rituals.
How you sprang away from my heart,
shredding my airy nightwings.

Shall I tell you of my life
yoked between a singing heart and doubting
mind, where truth is far from any frontier
and perception inverts
the linearity of atoms?

And how you, now,
running with tiger stride
hurry away from my love

still terrified and inwardly
unfocussed?

Reaction

For P.G.

It is evening now.
The trees are stubbornly silent,
a graceful bird thrills the churning heart.
It is the heart that sutures.
Legs weaken, lungs
fill with trembling,
wistful mind parades
a lingering sadness.

You caused me to worry today,
shattered my secret trump card
pieces lodged in your apartment corners.

(Beware of my fury.
It may still haunt your dreams.)

Uninvited, I came to meet
your darkness, a snake
denuded of its venom.
Held myself stubborn,
before your dragon eyes.

Erecting a wall of mist
you pried through my curtains,
without disturbing the lighting.

I trembled my palm
for the things I lent you

your silence forgetting
my presence.

Having done my doleful work
I turned away from your
vengeance, to the street
ablaze with treesongs,
to my children's
smiling innocence.

Walking up First Avenue, New York

For Diggers

The soft relic sun beats into my walking,
it is a Monday of roses and wondrous books.
Weaning myself from New York
like weaving naked
rubies into nightsky,
the pain, the edges of hands ,
the downward walking marking spaces.
Umbrellas dance to noontime rhythms
as parsley eyed as smiling Mondays.
It is not far now, the demonstrations
up ahead — Nicaragua,
El Salvador, Viet Nam
(co-opted by chemical warfare)
seeking pathways to American dream
sequences. I take the pamphlets and stuff
them in my pocket, where my heart
stays. Words do not recoil
in the satin stepping of filtering
banners. These are the unresolved
parables of a lost nation: errant
princess of midnight twilights,
cavorting in fear and restlessness,
in asphyxiated mythologies: Super mom,
America, Superman, the president, Super race,
the democratic-republican lineage.
New York as heartcentre of visions.
Macho. White and Blue. Repeated
in the New York sunshine

Parabolas of puzzled antennae among
nervous logarithms of peace conferences,
cheap havens of megalomania.

Dreaming of love, we lie naked on balconies
sucking in wordblooms, growing fat
on propaganda, longing for love.
In a patch of sweet grass, savage devas
collect the green from the mountain caverns
of New York apartments. Greenspeaking fences
become decadent signposts
for what used to be nature and good.
The grass grows thin
under the curious eyes of sidewalk
dwellers. I have walked thirty blocks
or more, 9000 years too far,
more sunshine than I can take in,
and answers still elude
the flight of flowers.
Azaleas in magenta gowns,
bespeak the hardness of silence,
the rot, the damned return
for nothing,
the steps
awaking in me
away from
away
away
ab
a

Lost Words

Her writing had touched me deeply, set my soul free.

Without understanding from where the stories came she wrote and wrote until well past eighty. Spindly threads of long stories appeared through her hands as she washed the supper dishes. Names leapt out at her, grimacing and ducking as she clipped the crooked hedge by the peeling garage; its blueness blurring into evening light. The stories never came as she wanted them but shaped themselves freely. They reminded her of the fragile refrain in the infrequent letters from old friends, "Youth like fire lasts only as long as the immortality of our thoughts," they wrote. She imagined word trickles falling from their pens into variegated silences, veridian abysses where Persephone's voice still roams across the orb of time seeking friends among living souls.

Always patient, the stories waited for her to hear their murmuring voices. Even the loud ones, sometimes weakened from their struggle to be heard, continued to whisper around her psyche with the stubbornness of cooling breezes.

Occasionally, the stories constructed themselves into vivid images dancing slowly in her inner ear, moving round and round, like longdancers who, without an audience, dance woefully around a lone tree through a long night; dancing towards the end of time, folding the echoing strains of humanity, into each difficult step.

Whenever she entered the cave of her creative source, the writer saw many images — strong, wily ones that sharpened her inner eye with violet light — glowing visions that unveiled plots to complex stories. Sometimes, they shouted and beckoned. Then she would rush around, looking for scraps of paper, blue, white, lined, soft or crumpled — more carefully choosing the right pen among the many that waited like patient servants for the tea bell of their dowager mistress.

Her writing flowed soundlessly, oracular, as she listened to the music of the inner voice floating along frenzied waves dictating the flesh and soul of the story.

The strong sun, hiding its ancient wrinkles behind an infinite mask of light, watched as she wrote hour after hour in a shaded corner of her garden or at her oak desk in the upstairs study; she wrote on and on, shoulders bowed over her enormous desk, sheltered from wafting breezes climbing through the open window. Often the moon, peered in, like a nosy neighbour who can't quite see through the brambles, sighing and whispering as night shadows uncovered brilliant stars.

Without fatigue, in a wild frenzy, as if in a trance she wrote day after day, month after month, often forgetting to eat and drink, neglecting the phone and the infrequent invitations of friends. Pages filled up with words, sentences, moods, characters — hypersensitive beings whose lives, carved from the sinews of complex vocabulary, birthed through the bone of grammar and the blood of syntax created New Worlds.

Her craft became her life. Dusty rooms filled with the sound of swaying trees shedding superfluous summer leaves. People breathed and grew old and sometimes died. Outside her window, cats meowed as far away soldiers planned vile attacks on unsuspecting villages, while newspapers cried out the evil news that no-one wanted to hear but everyone rushed to read.

I can almost see her working, see her hunched over the pages, struggling to keep awake.

She writes through tunnels of time. Time catches its breath.

The Acropolis decays stone by stone. The pyramids hold their stubborn secrets along labyrinthine tunnels. Someone casts the I Ching crying at the answer clothed in cryptic metaphors. Down the street, Pericles is seduced by the shrill caw of a blackwinged crow spilling early news into the morning quiet.

Sleep comes to the writer in these early hours when the streets are calm and the moon dreams behind curtains of clouds.

Time hums old tunes. Boxes fill up with paper: manuscripts of stories and poems, some half finished.

Eventually, the writer's hands begin to age; skin turns waxy, like gnarled tree bark that has weathered many winters. Fingers stiffen and harden under the soft touch of young lips. Even her speaking voice becomes quiet. Her wild brown eyes blur, lose their ability to see life's careful edges. Life, sleep and work fill the flow of days.

Daily, she edits and polishes her work, helping her stories take human form and walk, unaided, among people.

She tires easily now, and new stories creep around her like silent children coming out of their room after being sent to bed. Often, she feels the unbearable restlessness of poems begging to be let out, to be free, to be heard. Slowly she unlocks their silver boxes, carefully polishes and re-shapes their dusty bodies, occasionally fitting one or two into white envelopes which she mails out to the few magazines that still publish poetry and are glad to have them.

Over time, her heart becomes weary, her solitude deepens becoming indigo and feathered.

During sunny walks she hears the muffled, steady steps of death stalking her. She sighs and keeps walking, her keen eyes ever watchful.

Corridors grow darker. In the desert, the eternal Sphinx closes her eyes and sleeps, her secrets safe in her belly. Valiant seekers try to penetrate her silence, set up stethoscopes by her paws, hoping to uncover the knowledge buried deep within her spirit. Only the unfettered circulation of hope keeps the Sphinx's heartbeat from stopping. At night, the writer speaks to the Sphinx along starry highways linking her northern garden to the wild blue desert where the stony Sphinx lies dreaming — her mysterious feet bathed in the roots of her watery beginnings. The writer knows the Sphinx's secrets. They have become hers.

On quiet evenings, sometimes in summer, a deeper longing besieges the writer's memory. Through foggy time-lines, like someone living a walled city, she retraces the streams of her life, the many roads she has walked to get here, tracing the merging roads into a matrix of forgetting. More and more she barely recalls the tirades of her youth. They have become mythological events snaking through her consciousness. Nightly, as time grows longer, she conjures up more stories and trembles, like Moses before the Babbling Godfire. She fears being burned by their bluish embers.

Even as a young child, she knew that stories could burn the skin, singe the eyelashes, scald the toes, burnish the tapestry of her soul. She remembers sitting wide-eyed, burning, at her grandfather's travelled feet, listening to his voice, bravely navigating the shadows of flickering firelight to the other side of sleep as his voice waned and died in her ear: the old tales ebbing and flowing into her cup of memory.

Each night as the room grew colder, he told her another story, each breath revealing another marvel, another chapter.

Falling asleep at his knee, purple smoke swirling around his white moustache, she dreams of brown eyed kangaroos with empty pouches, black swans, sleeping princesses and herself, in ragged clothing, running, frightened through a dense forest hoping to glimpse a light through the thickly wooded path. There it is, just ahead, the lonely light of a tiny hut, holding out the uncertain promise of a warming fire, the comfort of a straw bed and a kind voiced crone whispering secrets.

Evil never entered into her living dreams. Ever.

Time took away her colour. Her hair became silvery, her eyes turned within. Her earthly dreams weakened, emptied of their former fire, until one day she fell asleep.

They found her at her walnut table, frosty head resting on an open notebook, thin shoulders covered with a green shawl whose fringes sheltered her written words with pale, silken fingers. Her last story lay unfinished but her lost words, electrical currents moving across the quilted page, still travel the eternal river of seeing, singing their stories in wild blue voices.

Anna

For Anna Harvey

Anna is a blue scented fir. She dances
through the wind's bright hair as it catches
and curls in her wide branches. High up
on the jagged mountainside, near a knotted knurl,
she looks down on valleys and lakes,
bluegreen eyes filled with the sounds of life.
She has been here for centuries,
always patient always wise:
listening for Spring's early sounds,
longing for the silent fugues of winter snows,
sheltering her in white robes.
She welcomes steamy, summer nights
and cool, autumn days. Her belly
holds the memory of time
and the quiet roads of the world
where the wind blows and thunders.
She has heard many stories,
remembers all the myths.
Her light sparkles through inner worlds
where her sacredness is known
where her name is chanted
in the ceaseless songs of crickets.

Starhorses Edging Earthlight

For D.P.

At night
the moon
holds me in her belly
I am small and cool
my eyes shiver like stars,
oboe starlight
pierces the pure
lunar womb,
kneading
tendrils of flesh
into wide winged rhythms.

I invent myself
in mothlike radiance,
salmon wings unfurl
in plumed flight
over moongold hills
and valleys,
a lilting spur of light
ascending to watery
silences
in the luminous
trance of cosmic
sounds: whales singing
in masts of mists,
rosaries of wolves
in howling forests.
I stalk the fitful

fate of friends,
who have traded
starhorses for a pension,
furrowed brows,
and days of forgetfulness.

My heart in flight,
I take refuge
in the saxe blue dawn
caped in cherry singing
fire, knurling
in her fiery pyre
the mighty dreams
of those who
nightly gather
on starhorses
edging
earthlight.

Pebbles

earthbones
fleshless
as the broken
air
sacrament of time
particles of colour
shaping
an ancient beach
touching my eye
with seeing

Pauline Johnson's House

Dark green shutters
white wood walls
shimmering forest
around
a single pine
lawn
scented with
sweetgrass.

Not faraway
dancing
tribes
drumming
voices
chanting
their history.

People
at crossroads,
invoking
lost timewaves.

Ancient sounds
forging
new spaces,
under
the indigo
wings
of hurrying
ravens.

Briefing for a Muse . . .

The dream archetype: a small boat carrying me across a lake, threatening to break up under the thunderous pounding of huge blue waves. I am hanging on to the edges, hovering above the image, wanting to see the whole thing. Yet some part of me stays in the scene glimpsing the details, writing its script.

The sky is a large mouth where clouds move. Dark birds and sun swim in a spacious copperblue dome.

I am a pasteboard cutout on a flat blue page. An image captured from a dream. I begin to move across the page in a tiny, yellow boat; water flows from right to left, imperfect wavelets gaining rhythm and momentum among shimmering waves.

The boat and my eye are one. The sea thunders and moans, the sky darkens. I move to the centre of the image, hover close to the page, animated by the seeing eye of my pen.

As the writer of this piece, I allow myself to be the person in the scene and the watcher at the edge of the postcard image, identifying with the moving picture and the core of the unfolding drama, not knowing what the words will say next.

A briny sun withdraws from the waves. Strong armed winds push the little boat further into the darkening sea.

I move my pen across the page following its movements. Windy arms filled with the weight of my words order the flight of images on the page: nouns, adjectives, tense of verbs and syntax arranging rhythm and text, hand moving from left to right and right to left. Again and again. Patient and determined.

Then, without warning, the boat, moving under the protection of my words, begins to spin, buffeted by the wilderness of my failing imagination. A pause. Hand stops. Pen wanders through the critical mind.

Images fade, words slur and whimper.

"Feel," screams the woman clinging to the sides of the boat. "The boat is large enough to hold me but not strong enough to withstand the coming storm of your doubt, the distortion of your critical thoughts." Her warning eyes glaze over, peer at me from the centre of the churning waves. She begins to slide into oblivion. The air around her is howling and I can barely hear her. Seabirds mouth empty sounds against thundering, godlike waves. The sea's flecked body like a luminous sky creature from an ancient tale, unfolds its serpent body, rises up to frighten her, roaring with the dark fury of crowds before the terror of an unknown power.

I feel our pain and whimper.

She who is stuck in the tiny, unsure boat can no longer hear anything. Almost deaf, brine burning her throat and blinding her eyes, she puts her fate firmly in my hands.

I still hesitate. Logic burns through my mind like a slow acid.

Lost and lurching in the cavernous wave mouths, buffeted by the pull and tug of a thousand winds, her boat rises, cresting the pillaging waves that uncoil like the demonic tail of a dragon. Swiftly, the winds move in, pulling it down, trying to drown it in the fall of waves, intent on burying furious claws into the skin of the woman's last hope.

A bird, white and soaring above the uncertain boat notices her frozen fear. Taking pity, it drops her a petal of hope.

As the feather of hope falls, my creator revives. My imagination spurs the drowsy pen. With Buddha like compassion, my pen hurries to rescue the image. Plot the story.Waves soften and sigh, bunch up into solid slides of water, easing the boat forward, calming the storm's impossible fury. Slowly, the boat moves across the waves climbing out of the storm's contentious roar. My sanguine pen scratches onward, in heroic silence, calming the storm's angry voice, groping hopefully, unhurried, for the immutable safety of the distant shore.

Oshawa Afternoon

For John Seed

I

Proud winter snows
in sleeping summer fields.
A frozen afternoon retreats
to a naked landscape
outside my window seat.

The rape of men
on this fluid land
echoes the pallor
of muted trees,
attaining the purity
of a Picasso sketch
on a whitewashed
Spanish wall.

Cold winter breath
seethes through
my wizened boots
as the train speeds on.

I weep for the terror
of dying trees,
for the secret
sleep of hills and
tortured grasses.
I seek the answer
to the riddle

on a passing billboard:
PRIME INDUSTRIAL SITE FOR SALE.

Its message haunts my soul,
the sales pitch obvious:
"The development of an industrial paradise
undertaken by the technological
impregnation of the ripened
womb of a virgin land."

"We will gouge out the trees in fury
plug up the rivers in a hurry
mortgage, parcel and deliver
the lilting curve of soft valleys
at no extra cost."

"No frogs or wildflowers
to clog up your sewers
no trees to absorb
your pollution.
We will honour
our bargain to the end
to the very bitter end
of civilised progress."

II

No blade of grass remains
under the torn billboard.

Windy silences fill the endless air,
caress the frozen bulrushes
waiting for their end.

A litany of sounds
roars through the train tracks.
An old nightmare
freezes in my hand.

And only the pain remains:
a painted word,
a silent whisper,
the dying eyes
of a martyred land,
shaping the voice
of this poem.

I Smile

For Walt Whitman

I smile for the sylphic sun
and the day for which it grows,
for the limpid rocks
and craggy brooks
that inhabit the quiet
places inside.

I smile for the bridge of rain
on sleeping clouds,
for the saturn moon
eclipsing my words,
and the touching,
weaving symphonies
circling your soul
so far away.

I smile for happy children
dancing in windblown fields:
a tide of love hugging my knees.

I sing litanies
around winter fires,
for the moustached storyteller
who nourished my childhood.
For the fresh new hope
that breaks into each morning
silencing the patterns of war
in our shattered hearts.

I sing for crying babes
and the briny wings of seagulls,
for the ebb and flow of crickets
in summer's fiery tongue,
singing through hours.

I sing with seasoned voice
under a dove faced sun,
living and dying in sameness
releasing the spirit.

And I sing for you
my children and my friends.
though life's candle burns
through my fingers
as I reach to put out the night.

Easter 1990

It is always the same conversation.
I fall in love with flowers and learn
to love everything about the sky.
I begin to adore the colour of new grass
and end up making love with autumn stars.
I breathe in and fall deeply in love
with my bones and the way they
co-operate in holding me together.
I fall in love with angels and they bring me gifts,
scattering grace all over my living room floor.
Spiders find me floating through windowpanes.
Crowds of songbirds sing petulant songs
     to a five o'clock sky.

My heart burns on.
And when I fall in love with people
it is never the same: a newborn child or her fragrance
unmask my heart. Green eyes looking through
     innocence
disarm my earthly masks. And when I fall in love
     with you
the poet hiding in my words caresses me with a fine
intuition, binding me to a helix of phrases, until
even my dreams enter the eternal narration.
And when I fall in love with cadence
poetry, like light recalls the lilting
sound of desert rain.

Psychobiography

Born fair of skin
bearing the
ominous name
of a warring angel:
Isa,
God
bella,
war,

of smouldering passion
I am made,
the swaddling
is made of time
the purpose to be learned
in the moment
of each encounter.

Through images of days
I am recreated,
a child
learning
to remember
the face
the shape
the ancestry
the once touched lovers
the windy afternoon
under your eyes.

The ocean spray of words
at the end of the tunnel.
The mirror darkness within.

I spin a new word.
Sound discovers wavelength.
Time is revolution.
Movement is being.

Finally, I arrive at myself,
and I no longer know you,
the other fairskinned woman.